My Pet Peepelo

story by
ELLIS CREDLE

photographs by
CHARLES TOWNSEND

OXFORD UNIVERSITY PRESS
New York   1948

THURSDAY was always a great day in Tacopan, a little village high up in the mountains of Mexico, for Thursday was market day. Everybody arose very early on Thursdays before the sun was up. They put on their best clothes and went down into the city in the valley to sell things in the market place, to hear about all the happenings of the week and to buy things they needed.

Little Tivo felt very sad on market day. He was not allowed to go down into the valley with the rest. He had nothing to sell and no money to buy things, and everyone knows that little boys with nothing to do are likely to get into mischief.

But on Thursdays he always got up as early as anyone else. He helped his mother cut great bunches of flowers to sell. He helped his father load the donkey with firewood to peddle in the town.

Then he waved them good-by as they started down the steep path with their neighbors. Down the mountain they wound, the men trotting beneath great crates of vegetables, the women loaded with gay flowers and fruit, and here and there among them a small donkey, stepping along beneath his two huge packs of wood or charcoal.

Tivo watched until they were out of sight. Then he felt very lonely. If only he had a little money! It would be wonderful to go down to town and buy himself a fine new hat, a red balloon or a beautiful new blanket to wear.

Then Tivo turned back to the house. He brought water for the pig and the calves and the chickens. After that, the day dragged.

At nightfall, Tivo's mother and father came home, tired and happy. They told him about all the things they had seen in the town, about the great cathedral with a tall golden altar and a beautiful Virgin with a jewelled crown, and about the brass band playing underneath the trees in the great square. They had bought a new kind of sandal made of old rubber tires that would keep one from slipping on the steep mountain paths. There had been fireworks in honor of St. Teresa's birthday.

Tivo listened eagerly. "Oh, mother!" he cried, "I do so want to go to the market!"

"You must wait until you have something to sell," said his mother. "Something you have made with your own hands or something you have raised by your own work."

For several days Tivo thought and thought. Then he went to his mother. She was grinding corn on the stone metate to make tortillas.

"If you would let me have a little bit of land, I could raise some vegetables to take to the market," said Tivo.

"The land belongs to the village," said his mother, shaking her head. "Our share is only lent to us for as long as we need it. Papa uses it all for growing our corn and beans. Think of something else."

For several days Tivo thought and thought but not an idea came to him. Then one day while his mother was at the village washtubs doing the family washing, along came the old mother turkey leading a downy baby turkey.

Tivo ran to tell his mother about it.

"She has hatched only one baby!" cried Tivo's mother. "Then she need not bring him to me to raise. She can just take him away and raise him herself!"

"But turkey mothers are so foolish!" said the other women at the tubs. "If you leave the little one with her, she will surely take him into the woods where the animals will eat him or she will lead him into the brook where he will drown."

"I cannot help it," replied Tivo's mother. "Baby turkeys are a great trouble to raise. You have to hunt them up and take them in when it rains; you have to keep them warm when it is cold; you have to feed them. For a whole brood of turkeys it would be worth the trouble, but for only one turkey—no!"

"Oh, mother, let me have the little turkey," spoke up Tivo. "I will gladly feed him and take care of him."

"You may have him and welcome," she replied.

"Oh, thank you, mother!" cried Tivo. "And when he is grown may I take him down to town and sell him in the market place?"

"Indeed, you may," promised his mother; "and you shall have the money to spend as you like. But I warn you, little turkeys are very hard to raise."

But Tivo was not easily discouraged. He ran home again. "Come, Peepelo, little turkey," he called gently, as he spread cornmeal upon the floor for the baby's dinner.

The little turkey looked at it for a moment with one beady black eye, then peck-peck-peck went the tiny bill, and it was not long before the meal was all gone.

Never was a little turkey better cared for. When Tivo had his breakfast in the morning, he took Peepelo upon his knee and fed him beans and tortilla from his own plate. At the first sight of rain, Tivo put on his raincoat made of palm leaves and ran to find his baby. He kept him in the house until the last drop had fallen.

Peepelo grew round and plump and friendly. He was like one of the family. At meal time he came stepping into the kitchen, peeping loudly for his dinner. At night, warmly wrapped in a piece of an old blanket, he slept on the foot of Tivo's bed.

And when the day for blessing the animals came around, Tivo made a beautiful wreath of flowers for Peepelo's neck and took him to the village church. Many people were there with their animals—men with pigs and oxen and donkeys and cows, all garlanded with flowers; women with chickens and turkeys and geese; their feathers stuck with blossoms; children with their pcts—dogs, cats or roosters—dyed pink or green or yellow for the occasion.

"Peepelo is the prettiest one of all," Tivo said to himself, as he stood in line with the rest.

The good Padre stood at the church door and blessed each bird or beast as it was brought past him. Everyone went home happy, feeling sure that his animal or fowl would live and be healthy for another year.

How Peepelo grew after that! His legs got long and gangling. He lost the baby down and became ragged and bare. He shivered in the cold morning mist, and in the evening he peeped unhappily.

"What shall I do?" wailed Tivo. "My little turkey has no feathers to keep him warm. He is so cold! Can't you make him a little blanket, mother, a little blanket like mine to keep him warm on cold mornings?"

"I'll try," replied his mother, and she knitted a little blanket. It was gray with white and blue around the neck and it was just the right size for Peepelo. After that the little turkey ran around merrily behind the cactus fence with his friends the goat, the pigs, and the calves. He did not feel cold even on the chilliest mornings.

Then a few weeks later, his feathers began to appear and he did not need his blanket any more.

He was a fine half-grown turkey now and he began to feel the urge to see the world. He explored the grove of banana plants behind the house, the cornfields on the hillside, and at last one day he ventured onto the wild rocky plains beyond.

"Don't you dare go out there, you foolish little turkey!" cried Tivo. "There is a ruined hacienda there where dangerous animals lurk. Long ago it was a great walled castle, they say, and many men worked there for the Spanish master, but now it is all deserted. Foxes live in the holes and wildcats hide in the broken walls. They will catch you and eat you up!"

But Peepelo was full of curiosity. What juicy grasshoppers he found in the ruined courtyards! How many fat crickets there were among the bushes! He ran happily here and there. Suddenly he caught sight of two gleaming eyes. They were staring at him over a crumbling wall. Something told Peepelo this meant danger. He spread his wings and began to run. A bobcat leaped from the wall and ran after him.

Peepelo, glancing backward, could see a red tongue and shining eyes. The cat leaped forward. His jaws closed on Peepelo's tail feathers.

Peepelo squawked with terror. He beat his wings and dug his toes into the ground but he could not pull away. Tired and hopeless, he was about to give up when he heard someone calling, "Peepelo, Peepelo, where are you, Peepelo?" It was Tivo coming to find him.

With a peep of joy, Peepelo jerked with all his might. Some of his tail feathers came away in the bobcat's mouth, and away fled Peepelo. He sped along toward the friendly voice.

Tivo saw his pet flying for his life. He ran to him and snatched him up. The disappointed bobcat stole away among the cacti.

"You see! What did I tell you?" cried Tivo. "In a moment the bobcat would have eaten you!"

Peepelo never went to the hacienda again. In the mornings when Tivo was helping his father in the cornfields, he trotted at his heels. He scratched for worms or picked up the grains of corn that were dropped when the ears were pulled from the stalk. At noontime when Tivo went home from the fields, Peepelo ran behind. When they got home, Tivo took him up, stroked his feathers, carried him into the house and gave him a part of his own dinner.

Peepelo was growing to be a handsome young turkey now. His tail had grown out again. The feathers around his neck had fine white designs. A fine red wattle hung smartly from his beak. He learned how to spread his tail into a beautiful fan and parade proudly before the chickens and the barnyard animals.

"Look, Tivo," said his mother. "See how your turkey struts! He is fully grown now. If you want to take him to the market, now is the time. He is young and plump and tender."

Tivo thought of all the beautiful things to be bought in the market place. "Oh, mother," he cried, "may I go with you next Thursday?"

"Yes, indeed you may," replied his mother.

On the very next Thursday when the sky was pink with the sunrise, Tivo and his turkey joined the little procession that went trooping away from the village of Tacopan. Peepelo nestled comfortably underneath Tivo's arm with his head stuck out so that he might see the sights as they passed along.

Down from the high mountains they wound, down from the cool mountain air, the dark cedar and pine trees. What wonders Tivo saw along the way! He lagged and lagged behind. When they passed a great pyramid of stone, he stared at it with wonder. "What is that, mama?" he cried, running after her.

"It is something our people built long ago before we were conquered by the Spaniards. They say it was a temple for worshipping the sun."

"Why did they worship the sun, mama?"

"They worshipped it because it makes the plants grow. It is the giver of all life. Without it everything would die. It was their god."

At a turn in the road Tivo lifted his eyes and saw a great mountain peak towering into the sky. Its top was glittering white with snow.

"Look! There is old Popo!" papa said, pointing toward it. "Always and forever there is snow on the top. Deep down inside it there is a fire—a great rumbling fire. Sometimes the smoke pours from the top as from a giant chimney! Popocatapetl it has been called since ancient times."

"Popocatapetl, Popocatapetl," Tivo repeated the long name.

On and on they trudged away from the great volcano.

They came within sight of the town at last. How beautiful it was with the pink stone towers of the church pointing into the blue sky and the rose tile roofs of the houses shining among the green trees!

Tivo had never seen so many beautiful houses—snowy white ones, cream-colored ones, blue ones. Many had beautiful carving around the doors and windows. Red and purple flowers climbed over the roofs, and palm trees waved in the breeze. Tivo walked slower and slower looking at the strange new sights.

They passed along the street to the church.

At last they came to the market place. Oh, what splendid things were there! So many fine things that Tivo could not decide which he wanted most. Vegetables everywhere! Hats in one stall, blankets in another, fancy pots and jars piled along the sidewalk, a stall full of all sorts of wonderful toys. A man stood on the corner with a handful of balloons that bobbed in the breeze. Another, whose tray was piled up with bright-colored candy, wandered here and there, shouting his wares. Everybody was busy and smiling.

Tivo could hardly decide where to look first. At last he stopped at the toy counter.

"Hi there, little boy!" the toy-seller called out to him. "Look at this fine horseman made of straw! Here is a beautiful pig with flowers painted on him. Here is a little guitar that makes a nice tune. Look at this mask! Put it on your turkey. How terrifying he looks! Now he can join the dancers at the festival of our lady of Guada-loupe!"

How funny Peepelo looked! Tivo laughed with de-light, but Peepelo gobbled indignantly.

"And look at this fine monkey," said the toy-seller. "See how he climbs the stick! Here, try it yourself. Did you ever see anything funnier than that?"

He put the climbing monkey into Tivo's hand. Tivo pulled the string as the man showed him. It made the monkey go climbing up the stick. Oh, what fun! Tivo laughed aloud. He would never grow tired of playing with a toy like that!

"How much is it?" he asked the toy-seller.

"It's only two pesos," said the toy-seller. Then, bend-ing down, he whispered into Tivo's ear. "But if you haven't got that much, I might let it go for one."

"I will come back and get it in a little while—as soon as I sell my turkey," said Tivo.

The toy-seller nodded. "Don't wait too long or it might be sold."

Tivo's mother was sitting in the market place selling her flowers. Tivo sat down beside her. "Where shall I sell my turkey?" he asked.

"Try over there," said his mother, pointing down the street toward a woman who was selling food at a side-walk stand.

Tivo walked toward her. "Remember," his mother called after him, "ask fifteen pesos for your turkey. If she bargains with you, you can come down to ten. That is a fairly good price."

"Yes, mother," Tivo called back.

"Hi there, sonny!" The woman looked up from the great pot she was stirring. "How much will you take for that turkey?"

"Fifteen pesos," said Tivo.

"Oh, that is too much! I will give you ten. Is it a bargain?"

Ten pesos! Enough to buy the monkey with something left over for candy or a balloon. What luck! Tivo held out his turkey, then slowly he drew him back. Suddenly he felt it was not very important to have the climbing monkey. "Peepelo can do tricks too," he said to himself. "He can balance himself on the foot of my bed and sleep there all night. What could be cleverer than that?" Indeed, he was much cleverer than that monkey that had to be worked with a string!

"Well, well!" said the woman impatiently, holding out the ten pesos. "Don't you want to sell your turkey?"

"I may sell him later," murmured Tivo, "but not right now."

The woman laughed good-naturedly as she turned back to her pot.

Tivo hurried away. When his mother saw him coming back with the turkey still under his arm, she said in surprise, "Why didn't you sell him? Wouldn't she give you a good price?"

Tivo said nothing. He looked very unhappy.

"Well, try the weaving-man in that house over there. He might want a fowl for turkey molé."

The weaving-man was busy at his great wooden loom.

"Do you want to buy a turkey?" asked Tivo. "For turkey molé?"

"Ah! Turkey molé!" exclaimed the weaving-man with a happy smile. "Delicious hot sauce poured over a nicely cooked turkey! Those old Aztecs knew what they were about when they invented molé sauce!" Then his face became gloomy. "But nowadays I can't afford to buy turkeys—people do not buy my blankets as they once did. The machines in the factories are making them now, faster and cheaper than I can. I do not make much money. No, I am afraid I cannot buy your turkey, little boy."

Tivo returned to his mother. "The weaving-man couldn't buy him."

"Well, try the butcher," his mother said. "His shop is over there. It's the one with the big picture painted on the wall."

Tivo wandered along toward the butcher-shop. On the way he passed a stall where blankets were sold. There was a beautiful one hanging right in front and he stopped to admire it.

"Try it on!" urged the stall-keeper and slipped it over Tivo's head.

My, but it was a fine blanket—gray with red and white designs around the neck and around the border. Tivo strutted a little.

"How much is it?" he asked.

"Ten pesos," said the stall-keeper. "And there isn't a finer blanket in all of Mexico!" Then bending down to Tivo's ear, he whispered, "Since you are a little boy and I want to make you happy, I might sell it for nine pesos, but don't tell anybody."

"As soon as I sell my turkey, I will come back and get it," said Tivo. Taking the blanket off, he marched firmly away to the butcher-shop.

What a funny picture there was on the wall outside the butcher-shop!

"Just look at that!" Tivo said to Peepelo. "The pig is weighing the man. I suppose he's going to cut him up and sell him for meat."

Just then the butcher came out and saw the fine fat turkey.

"How much do you want for that bird, young fellow?" he asked.

"Fifteen pesos," said Tivo.

"I'll give you eleven," said the butcher. "Is it a bargain?"

Eleven pesos! He could buy the blanket and there would still be enough left over for the climbing monkey. How wonderful! The butcher held out the money.

Tivo looked down at his pet. How beautifully his feathers shone in the sunlight! What lovely white designs there were around his neck! Surely that blanket he had tried on was not half so fine! No, it was not half so fine! And he felt now that he did not want it at all. He backed away from the butcher.

"I think I will not sell my turkey just now," he said.

The butcher smiled. "Money is not everything," he said, as he put the eleven pesos back into his pocket.

Tivo wandered through the market place. In front of the hat-stall he met his father.

"Haven't you sold that turkey yet?" asked his father.

"Not yet," confessed Tivo.

"Hurry up and sell him and buy yourself one of these fine hats," said his father.

Tivo looked at the hats. What beautiful ones there were, white ones, green ones, pink ones!

"Try this one," said his father, picking up a tall hat with a fancy leather band. "Not so long ago everyone in Mexico wore hats like this. They made a man look handsome and important."

Tivo put on the hat. How fine he felt with the broad brim curling up all around! The hat-seller looked at him admiringly and even Peepelo gobbled pridefully.

"How much is it?" Tivo asked.

"It's six pesos, a very fine hat!" said the hat-seller. Then, leaning over, he whispered softly, "But I might let you have it for five."

"If I could sell my turkey I would buy it," said Tivo.

"Have you tried the hotel?" asked the hat-seller, pointing to a large building with a great iron-grill gate. "That is where the Americans go. They are all rich and the hotelkeeper makes a lot of money. He will pay you well for your turkey."

Tivo walked across the square toward the hotel. He peered through the great gate into the patio. Birds were singing in cages, a fountain was tinkling and palm trees were rustling pleasantly in the breeze.

"What do you want, little boy?" asked the gateman.

"I have a turkey to sell," said Tivo.

The gateman swung the gate open.

Tivo entered the patio. A man came bustling forward. "Ah, you want to sell your turkey?" he asked. "How much?"

"Fifteen pesos," said Tivo.

"Fifteen pesos. Very well I will give you fifteen pesos."

Fifteen pesos! It was unheard of! He could buy the hat, the blanket and the monkey too!

The man held out his hands for the turkey. But Tivo, looking down at Peepelo nestling in his arm, felt all of a sudden that his pet was worth more than everything in the market put together. "I could not sell my turkey for fifteen pesos," he said.

"Well then, I will give you eighteen pesos, but it's an outrageous price."

Tivo slowly shook his head. "Not for eighteen pesos."

The man threw his hands into the air. "Get along with you," he cried, laughing. "You don't *want* to sell your turkey!"

Tivo found his mother and father packing up to go home.

"You couldn't sell your turkey?" exclaimed his father.

"There is no use to try anymore," said his mother, smiling a little. "I'm afraid we shall have to take Peepelo back home with us. We have only time now to stop in the cathedral a moment."

They crossed the square to the church. Tivo tied Peepelo to the iron fence, then through the huge carved doors they went. They knelt and prayed a moment, then sat looking up at the great golden altar. It was dim and hushed. High up, lit by a shaft of sunlight, stood the Virgin in a velvet dress and a jeweled crown.

Tivo gazed up at her through the dusk. Then he thought of his turkey waiting for him outside. "I am taking back from the market what I want most in all the world."

From her high place the Virgin seemed to smile down upon him approvingly.

The band was playing as they came onto the square again. Not far away some rockets began to flash into the sky. Flash! Flash! Flash! went the fiery streaks. Bang! Bang! Bang!

"Oh, they are having a fiesta!" mama cried. "It must be at the little church of San Juan on the road toward home. Hurry along and we'll be in time to see the fireworks!"

How beautiful it was on the way to the little church of San Juan! All across the street were arches of flowers. And many people carrying candles and armfuls of flowers were hurrying upward.

In the churchyard were dancers in bright costumes performing the olden dance of the Christians fighting the Moors. Their queer masks bobbed and nodded, their swords clanged against each other as they spun and jumped about. How exciting! Even Peepelo peeped with delight!

In the front of the church a castle of fireworks towered into the air. When they saw a man touch a match to it, Tivo and his mother and father climbed upon a hillside to watch.

"Here, scramble onto my shoulders!" cried Tivo's father as the fire sped up the pole. "Now you can see everything!"

Up went the fire from tier to tier. Wheels of red light spun round and round. A papier-mâché monkey jumped and danced as the firecrackers popped all around him. A bull kicked and plunged, trying to buck a bullfighter off his back, then exploded with a bang. An alligator opened his great mouth and swung his tail as he tried to swallow an iguana, then blew up with a roar. At the very top of the pole an angel whirled madly round and round, then suddenly unfolded golden wings and went whizzing off the pole high into the air. A shower of stars fell from her as she flew. Tivo was too delighted to speak.

"We must go home now," papa said at last. "It gets dark very quickly in the mountains."

Tivo gave a last look at the beautiful fiesta and they began the long trip over the mountains to home.

As they were having their beans and tortillas that night, papa glanced at Peepelo sitting on the back of a chair. "What a foolish boy to bring your turkey back home. If you had sold him you could have bought yourself a wonderful new hat, a blanket or a fine new toy."

"Oh, maybe not so foolish after all," his mother replied. "A boy gets tired of a toy very quickly, and a new hat or a new blanket soon seems to him like any other hat or blanket. But he never grows tired of something he loves. It is always new and wonderful to him."

Tivo held out a piece of tortilla to his turkey. "No, no I'll never grow tired of Peepelo," he said. "I'll always love my Peepelo!"

"Gobble! Gobble! Gobble!" said Peepelo joyfully.